LANCES AND CHANCES

AN AMETHYST'S WAND SHOP MYSTERIES STORY

LAURA GREENWOOD

ARIZONA TAPE

© 2023 Laura Greenwood

All rights reserved. This book or parts thereof may not be reproduced in any form, stored in any retrieval system, or transmitted in any form by any means – electronic, mechanical, photocopy, recording or otherwise – without prior written permission of the published, except as provided by United States of America copyright law. For permission requests, write to the publisher at "Attention: Permissions Coordinator," at the email address; lauragreenwood@authorlauragreenwood.co.uk.

Visit Laura Greenwood's website at:

www.authorlauragreenwood.co.uk

Visit Arizona Tape's website at:

www.arizonatape.com

Cover by Vampari Designs

Lances and Chances is a work of fiction. Names, characters, places, and incidents are the products of the author's imagination or are used fictitiously. Any resemblance to actual persons, living or dead, businesses, companies, events, or locales is entirely coincidental.

If you find an error, you can report it via Laura's website. Please note that our books are written in British English: https://www.authorlauragreenwood.co.uk/p/report-error.html

BLURB

A jousting accident leads to teaming up with an unknown detective...

When Amy and Ambrose arrive at a museum for a well-deserved day off, they find themselves pulled into an investigation they never saw coming, a jousting accident.

With plenty of witnesses, a dangerous sport, and no end of information, it seems like the case could be a simple open-and-shut one, even if it's not supposed to be their own.

But as more comes to light, they realise that what appears to be an accident, might not be as simple as they first thought.

-

Lances and Chances is a side story in the Amethyst's Wand Shop Mysteries urban fantasy murder mystery series. It involves a standalone crime. The events take place between Spells and Bells and Trials and Vials.

ONE

I LET out a loud sigh and slip my hand into Ambrose's, giving it a small squeeze.

He looks at me, a quizzical expression on his face.

"Don't look at me like that, I'm just excited that we're on a date that isn't going to get interrupted by murder," I say brightly.

He chuckles and raises an eyebrow. "You love murder."

"Hey, don't say that too loud, people will think I'm out there killing people. I'm not even armed."

"You're a witch, Amy, you're always armed."

"Yes, but I'm not going to use my wand like that, you know that."

"Other people don't," he teases.

I narrow my eyes at him. "Well, I'm looking forward to seeing some *real* weapons. Did you hear that they have the helmet of Henry VIII here? I've heard rumours that it's enchanted, do you think they're true?"

He shrugs.

"What about the elephant armour? Do you think that was really worn by a shifter?" I babble on excitedly.

"I'm sure there'll be a guidebook inside that tells us," he points out.

"Yes, but I want to know what *you* think," I remind him.

"I think that I love you."

I roll my eyes but feel warmth well up within me despite that. "You always love me."

"Except when you haven't had enough sleep," he teases.

"Charming," I mutter, but I'm stopped from saying anything else by the familiar sight in front of the museum doors.

A sight I did *not* expect to see today and have a surge of mixed feelings about. Police tape usually excites me but not when it's interfering with my date. And to make matters worse, the blue and white tape is stopping us from getting to the entrance of the museum so we can't even ask what's going on.

A grumpy woman with a gaggle of children behind her pulls a face and demands to speak to the manager, which makes me feel a little guilty about my thoughts. It's not the museum's fault that there's been a crime here. Or maybe it is. The place is full of weapons, after all. It's just asking for a big juicy murder.

I reach out to touch the tape, struggling to resist the urge to duck under it like I normally do at a crime scene but considering Ambrose and I have come to this museum as a date and not for work, it's highly inappropriate. Especially since we're outside our jurisdiction.

"Amy," Ambrose warns.

"But I wanted to see their new collection of mediaeval wands," I try to justify.

He gives me a look that says he knows *exactly* what I'm thinking, and that it's not about mediaeval wands, though I do want to see them. Maybe there's something I can learn about wandcraft from them.

Ambrose brushes his hand against my lower back. "Come on, let's go home."

"But we don't have a lot of time off, and we came all this way, it'd be a shame not to see anything." I play with the tape, trying to get a glimpse of what's happening on the other side. I can make out some of the red and blue lights of the police cars by the entrance and there are some people in uniform, but it's hard to tell what exactly is going on, or even if the uniforms belong to the Paranormal Police Department, or just the regular human kind.

The woman manages to convince the children that there's ice cream if they cooperate, but from her expression, I'm unsure how true that is.

The people on our other side mutter and wander off to one of the restaurants, leaving us alone by the tape.

"Do you think it's murder?" I voice out loud now that we're alone.

"Not everything is murder, Ames," he jokes.

"They have murders in Leeds. Oh, maybe something came to life." Both would be interesting and exciting possibilities.

A laugh falls from Ambrose's lips. "Your imagination knows no bounds. It could be all sorts of things. An accident, assault, kidnapping, theft, just processing a scene."

Despite his tone, he looks just as intrigued as I am. If I wait, he'll be the one pulling out his PPD badge and getting us into the scene. It's a good thing my consultant pass is in my handbag, though that's more through laziness than design.

Some of the uniforms move closer, and I catch sight of a familiar badge. PPD. It's a paranormal crime and that only makes it more intriguing. Unfortunately, they're still too far away to hear what they're saying. I feel like such a busybody but my curiosity is why I'm so good at consulting on murders. I just wish I could turn it off when it isn't needed.

Ambrose touches the tape and hums. "The barrier is magical though so whatever it is, it's paranormal in nature," he says, coming to the same conclusion. I suppose it makes sense when we're the ones still here, but the other people have been turned away. That's how magical police tape is meant to work.

"Is this where I suggest that you flash them your badge?" I ask as innocently as possible.

"Better not, the local detectives won't take kindly to me barging in."

A security guard comes from the building and comes our way with a stern but apologetic smile. "Sorry, folks. The museum is closed today. Sorry about that."

I don't want apologies, I just want to be able to

go inside and look at cool ancient weaponry. And whatever is going on inside.

"Did something bad happen?" I ask, unable to resist. "We were hoping to see the jousting tournament this afternoon. It was a special event, will they be redoing it?"

The guard struggles to keep his expression neutral. "I think the jousting tournament will be cancelled."

"The whole thing is cancelled?" I give Ambrose a look, suspicion rising inside me. I'm even more intrigued now but I don't want to be the person making a scene. As much as I want to be cheeky, everything I do reflects back on Ambrose and I don't want to become known as the unprofessional witch consultant.

"What else is there to do around here?" Ambrose asks politely.

"There are plenty of lovely restaurants and pubs around. If you're looking for something to visit, there's the butterfly house, or there's a science museum not far from here," the guard says, pointing out. "There's a map of the city just there."

It's disappointing to step away but those are the rules. We can't just barge in on any crime scene we see. It might not be anything interesting anyway.

my consultant pass is in my handbag, though that's more through laziness than design.

Some of the uniforms move closer, and I catch sight of a familiar badge. PPD. It's a paranormal crime and that only makes it more intriguing. Unfortunately, they're still too far away to hear what they're saying. I feel like such a busybody but my curiosity is why I'm so good at consulting on murders. I just wish I could turn it off when it isn't needed.

Ambrose touches the tape and hums. "The barrier is magical though so whatever it is, it's paranormal in nature," he says, coming to the same conclusion. I suppose it makes sense when we're the ones still here, but the other people have been turned away. That's how magical police tape is meant to work.

"Is this where I suggest that you flash them your badge?" I ask as innocently as possible.

"Better not, the local detectives won't take kindly to me barging in."

A security guard comes from the building and comes our way with a stern but apologetic smile. "Sorry, folks. The museum is closed today. Sorry about that."

I don't want apologies, I just want to be able to

go inside and look at cool ancient weaponry. And whatever is going on inside.

"Did something bad happen?" I ask, unable to resist. "We were hoping to see the jousting tournament this afternoon. It was a special event, will they be redoing it?"

The guard struggles to keep his expression neutral. "I think the jousting tournament will be cancelled."

"The whole thing is cancelled?" I give Ambrose a look, suspicion rising inside me. I'm even more intrigued now but I don't want to be the person making a scene. As much as I want to be cheeky, everything I do reflects back on Ambrose and I don't want to become known as the unprofessional witch consultant.

"What else is there to do around here?" Ambrose asks politely.

"There are plenty of lovely restaurants and pubs around. If you're looking for something to visit, there's the butterfly house, or there's a science museum not far from here," the guard says, pointing out. "There's a map of the city just there."

It's disappointing to step away but those are the rules. We can't just barge in on any crime scene we see. It might not be anything interesting anyway.

I let out a loud disappointed sigh.

"There'll be plenty of murders at home," Ambrose assures me.

"It's not just the murder," I murmur. "It's… Stacey?" I frown at the unmistakably pink-clad-lab-coat-wearing figure approaching us, with an equally familiar-looking guy trailing behind her.

"It's Stacey?" he asks, amusement in his tone.

I nod in the direction of my friend.

Ambrose turns, a smile lifting up the corners of his lips as he waves at the necromancer. "Doctor Barnes, Doctor Rook."

The two of them stop in their tracks and look at us.

"Ames? Ambrose? I didn't expect you here," Stacey says, my surprise aimed back at me.

"Likewise."

"What are you doing here?" she asks, ducking under the tape and holding it up for Gabriel Rook to pass beneath it. He reaches out and touches the small of her back.

"I'll start getting set up," he says softly.

She nods.

"We're on a date," I supply, eyeing up the tape and wondering about our chances of getting under it now we know the forensics team attending the scene. They do say it's who you know and not what you know. "What are you doing here?"

"There was a fatal accident, I was called in for the autopsy." Ah, one of her consulting cases. I know that she and Gabriel go on them fairly regularly, but I've no idea what they do on them. But that's not the important thing right now.

"I knew it! I knew there was a dead body." I know it's distasteful to be so excited about death but I like when my instincts are right.

Stacey chuckles. "Are you sure you're not part necromancer?"

"Nope. Full witch for seventeen generations of Amethysts," I point out. "Or more, I suppose Dad still counts as a generation, but he's not an Amethyst. Anyway, not important. I'm very witch," I ramble without meaning to.

"Who's in charge of the scene?" Ambrose asks.

Oh, good. My rebelliousness has caught onto him. He'd never even have considered asking a few years ago. I don't know if that's a good thing or not.

"Detective Celine DuFort. She's good," Stacey answers. "Do you know her?"

Ambrose shakes his head, but the name sparks hazy memories within me that I can't place. I don't know anyone outside our own station in the PPD, so I'm not sure what makes me think I know her.

"Any chance we can have a look?" I ask, crossing my fingers behind my back.

Stacey crosses her arms firmly. "I thought you two were on a date."

A bemused chuckle comes from Ambrose's direction. "She just wants to see the wand exhibit. She's been talking about it the whole drive here."

I gasp dramatically. "It's not just about the wands. There are several other exhibits I want to see, including the vampire hunting kit that I doubt has ever been used, and a collection of samurai swords said to be forged with dragon fire. But I also want to see the dead body," I add, knowing my friend will appreciate my honesty.

Ambrose smiles in bemusement, while Stacey nods approvingly. Maybe some people would find my enthusiasm strange, but Ambrose investigates murders for a living, and Stacey is quite literally a magical death being. One who also investigates murder for a living. Though maybe it could be said that she investigates murder for the dead. I resist the urge to laugh at my own joke.

"I can't officially invite you in on the case," she says looking between the two of us. "You know that's up to the detective, but I can make introductions," Stacey says, nodding at the security guard while she shows him her badge.

I allow myself a moment of glee as the tape lifts before I file it away. As excited as I am to get some answers, I'm not blind or insensitive. The moment we cross this barrier, it's like we're stepping on sacred ground. The person who died here deserves my respect, even if I know nothing about them.

TWO

I'VE NEVER BEEN to a death at a museum before, and I have to admit that I'm surprised by it, which is saying something. Having seen body parts sewn together, bodies dumped in playgrounds, and my sister's wedding cake baker dead on the floor of her own bakery, I thought nothing would surprise me.

I was wrong.

Everywhere I look, there are people. I don't think I've ever seen so many at a crime scene before, even when we've been dealing with serial killers, and I'm not sure what to make of it. I'm not surprised to see police agents, emergency personnel, or techs, but all the people in mediaeval clothes look out of place. From the dazed expressions on their faces, I'd guess that they're the witnesses.

"What happened?"

"No idea, I only just got here," Stacey points out. "But as far as I know, there was an accident while they were practising for the jousting tournament." She draws us through the pristine white halls.

"A jousting accident?" Ambrose echoes.

"That must be why the security guard said the whole tournament will be cancelled. How bad is it?" I ask, unsure how I feel about this. Is it going to be messy?

Stacey shakes her head. "I'm not sure. I haven't seen the body yet. We only just arrived when you two called my name."

For a moment, my gaze drifts to the huge staircase with weapons decorating the stairwell which leads to the exhibits. It's a reminder that the museum is full of potential murder weapons, from ancient, to most recent. Both magical and mundane. It's certainly an interesting place for a case. Not that we're officially on it. There might not even be a murder but that doesn't really matter to me. There's a mystery and that's all I want.

We move into the paranormal wing of the museum that's spelled to deter humans and pass a particular section that's just about wands and the old practices, most of which seem fairly standard still. I wish we had time to read all the plaques but there are more current affairs that need our attention.

"Do they know if it's an accident or could there have been foul play?" I ask.

Stacey gives me a look. "What part of '*I haven't seen the body yet*' didn't compute?"

I chuckle. "Sorry. I just thought they might have told you more."

"Friends don't keep secrets about murder," Stacey responds brightly. "You'd be the first person I'd tell if I killed someone."

"Should I feel bad for Gabriel that you're not telling him first?" I tease.

She snorts. "Who do you think I killed?"

I shake my head in bemusement, wondering just how much murder talk happens when they're home alone. Probably about as much as when Ambrose and I are alone. Though a lot of our conversation is also taken up by how much my parents are annoying Grammie, and whether Rover has been on his daily walks and had his dinner. The last one is normally accompanied by puppy eyes towards where we keep the dog food.

The glass doors slide open, revealing a surprisingly boring courtyard. A waft of a musky odour hits me in the face. It's just pure sweat and the smell of horses, sawdust, and metal polish. I'm not entirely sure I'd call it unpleasant, but I'm glad that I only have to smell it for a small amount of time. At least there aren't any horses around right now, but the hoof prints everywhere make it clear that that they were.

A woman in a brown pantsuit comes our way and pulls a blue glove off to shake hands with Stacey. "Hi, Doctor Barnes. Thank you for coming so quickly."

"Of course, Detective DuFort." Stacey gestures to us. "I'll make quick introductions. This is Detective Ambrose from the Hull PPD and his consultant, Amethyst—"

"From the Gemstone Coven," Celine DuFort finishes, her gaze lingering on me. "I remember."

So we *do* know each other. I'm just not sure from where.

I give her an embarrassed smile.

The woman chuckles as she points at herself. "Celine Celiac? I had much longer hair back then, all the way down to my waist."

Things click and I marry up the image of an old friend to the detective with the much shorter haircut and a few more laugh lines around the eyes. I suppose I probably have some too.

"Oooh, I do remember! Wow, sorry. It's just

been a while and I didn't recognise you without all the neon lights," I joke.

Celine lets out a sparkling laugh. "Tell me about it, daylight is a real vibe killer."

I look at Ambrose and put my hand on his arm, just to make it clear to everyone that I'm more than just his consultant. "Celine and I were part of the same LGBTQ club at the academy."

His face brightens. "Ah. Nice to meet you." He holds out his hand to her.

She shakes it. "Likewise. Ambrose, was it? Any relation to Commissioner Ambrose?"

I close my eyes and repress a groan, knowing he hates it when people make the connection. Though I suppose the alternative is for him to introduce himself as Detective Knight, and I know he'd hate that even more.

Ambrose nods. "He's my great-grandfather. We're not here on official business, we happened to pass by and got curious."

"Did someone really die while jousting?" I ask, my attention back on the reason why we're here.

Celine gives me a wry smile and gestures for us to follow her further into the courtyard. "That's what I thought when I heard it. My partner is off sick, and the department is heavily understaffed at the moment, so I wouldn't mind a second opinion. Since you're here and curious, that is." The expression on her face reveals that she knows what I'm like.

A man in a pristine suit peels himself away from Gabriel, who has somehow already gotten himself into one of the horrible white scene-of-crime suits in the time it's taken us to get here.

The man heads in our direction and holds out his hand to shake each of ours in turn. I study him intently, trying not to think about how weirdly out of place in the midst of all the mediaeval decor.

"I'm Hans Harding, I'm in charge here," he says. "Thank you for coming so quickly. We're all horrified by the situation and we'd like to get this sorted as quickly and quietly as possible."

Celine stiffens slightly but smiles. "We'll do our best. What can you tell us about the deceased?"

"Not much, I'm afraid. His name is Jeremiah Reese, he's part of the jousting team running the demonstration for us. You'll have to ask the rest of the team more about him."

Ambrose nods. "What about his opponent?"

"Umm…" Hans Harding fidgets with a clearly fake toupée. "Lars something, I think. Lars Baker. Again, I don't really know them. This is not something I'm in charge of, do you understand?"

Celine gives him a tight smile. "Understood," she

responds. "If there's anything else you can think of that we should know, please don't hesitate to call." She hands him her card.

He nods and hurries off.

"I don't like him," I murmur.

Stacey chuckles. "Good, because this is a suspicious death, even if it isn't murder. You shouldn't be trusting anyone but the body, and even that can lie." She strides off to where Gabriel is waiting with a SOCO suit for her.

"Is she always so cryptic?" Celine asks me.

"Not usually." Or maybe I'm just better at understanding my best friend than I think I am.

THREE

THE SCENT of horses grows stronger as we make our way to the centre of the courtyard, and from the piles of manure around, it seems obvious about the cause of it. I can't imagine they'd leave it lying around like this if there were visitors here, but they'll have had to leave the crime scene intact in order for us to properly investigate.

A wooden barrier separates the courtyard into two lengths but there's nothing on this side of it besides a lot of dislodged earth. My chest tightens as we make our way past the barrier, a familiar sensation whenever I know I'm about to come face-to-face with the deceased for the first time. As much as I enjoy unravelling the truth behind the deaths we investigate, this part never stops being horrific, especially when there's a hint of the unknown.

I stare at the tableaux before me, trying to make sense of what I'm seeing, and knowing that there's absolutely no doubt this death is going to stay imprinted on my mind for a long time to come. It isn't every day I see someone dead in full armour. The only thing missing is his helmet, which I assume has been taken off so they could check on how the poor guy was doing.

I come to a stop between Ambrose and Celine, realising that somehow I've become some kind of go-between, and I don't really know how.

Celine flips open a notebook similar to the one that Ambrose carries around. "Jeremiah Reese, thirty-one, mage. They were doing a practice run for the jousting tournament later. I haven't had much information yet but apparently, he fell off his horse and didn't get back up."

Interesting how she clearly had this information about him and the accident but still asked the manager. And by interesting, I mean useful. It's always good to see how people respond to questions and requests for information.

Stacey appears beside us in her crinkly SOCO suit. "Are you ready for me, Detective DuFort?" she asks.

Celine nods. "All yours, Doctor Barnes."

I frown, surprised and confused by the

interaction. It's not that either of them are doing anything weird, more that I'm used to more casual crime scenes where no one is going around saying *Detective This* and *Doctor That*.

Except for Ambrose when I first met him. I hope this doesn't mean he's going to go back to calling Stacey and Gabriel by their full names all the time. That could get old fast.

Stacey crouches down next to the man and examines him, touching his face and the part of his neck that's not covered by the chest plate. "It's hard to tell but if I was to hazard a guess, I'd say broken neck from the impact. I'd have to examine him properly to be sure, though. This armour could be hiding anything."

I wince just thinking about the collision and how it would feel being thrown off a horse. Looking at the man on the ground, there's an element of surreality that the previous cases I've worked on didn't have. I don't know if it's the jousting, the fact that he's dressed up, or the place we're in, but it feels like someone is going to yell 'cut' any moment and he'll get up.

I know it's not going to happen, but I still find a small part of me hoping that it will. I don't like the idea that this is how he died, even if I've seen some equally horrifying things in my time as a PPD murder consultant.

Celine nods. "Do you know where we can find Lars Baker?"

"I think Doctor Rook said he was over there." Stacey gestures to the building.

A young man waits behind the glass doors, and even from here, I can tell he's distraught. My instincts say that I shouldn't trust everything I'm seeing as the blanket truth, but even from this distance, I'm finding it difficult to believe that his emotions aren't real. He's likely in shock having seen this happen to someone he knows, and that will make it hard for him to cover up what he's feeling.

Which I guess is good news for us when it comes to trying to get straight answers out of him, and from the other jousters.

I take a deep breath and think through everything we know about the scene. Which is *a lot*. Certainly more than we normally do, and usually when we arrive at a crime scene, the killer isn't waiting in the next room to be interviewed. Nor are there quite so many witnesses. This is either going to be the easiest, if most bizarre, case we've ever worked on, or all of the information is going to make it really difficult to get any answers.

I hope it's the former.

"I'm going to speak with Mr Baker about the incident. He already looks overwhelmed so I think it's best if I do that alone," Celine decides, looking at me and Ambrose. She gestures around the courtyard. "There are a lot of eyewitnesses that still need to give statements and team members to talk to. Far too many for me to go through on my own. I'd appreciate it if you talked to some people. If you're up for it?"

"Will do," Ambrose agrees, nodding at me. Warmth spreads through me. He knows me well. Which I suppose isn't surprising considering we've been together for a couple of years now.

We leave Stacey to her examination and once we're far enough away that no one can hear, I gently touch Ambrose's sleeve to get his attention.

He turns to me, a curious expression on his face.

"We don't have to get involved, if you don't want to. We're here to have a break from work, not get sucked into another case," I say, though now we're part of this, I'm too curious to let it fully go.

Ambrose's smile lifts his lips. "Yes, but I can tell that you're intrigued."

"Are you telling me that you aren't too?"

"Of course," he responds. "And there's only really one person I want to spend time with anyway."

"If you're talking about someone other than me, you're going to be in real trouble," I quip.

He chuckles and looks as if he wants to draw me in to show me some affection, but refrains from it. Which is probably wise given the current situation. "I mean you."

"We're here, our plans fell in the water and I mean... death by jousting. That's unusual, isn't it? I wonder if it's on Stacey's murder bingo."

He chuckles. "I would be more surprised if it *wasn't* on her bingo card."

"Did you know that Gabriel actually had one made for her? It's hung on the wall in her flat."

Ambrose raises an eyebrow. "Dare I ask how many are ticked off?"

"Three."

"Hmmm, so there's the *two bodies, one coffin* case we worked on, then let's guess...the Frankenstein body?"

"No, apparently she thought that one was too unrealistic to be on the card," I respond.

"And she thought that *two bodies, one coffin* was more likely than a serial killer sewing different body parts together?"

I shrug. "We've worked on both cases," I point out. "I can't remember what the other two are, you'll have to ask her."

"I'll put it on the agenda for our next dinner party."

"That's not how dinner parties work," I counter.

He raises an eyebrow. "Then why do we keep inviting the people we work with?"

I snort. "Okay, fair point. We need to make more friends. Or just accept that we're going to be talking about murder over coq-au-vin for the rest of our lives."

"I don't mind the sound of that."

I shake my head in bemusement, but really, I love it.

"For what it's worth, I don't see the harm in helping out. I'll get to be the consultant for once, that's kind of neat.," Ambrose says, answering my original question.

"Ah, now you'll get to see why I love it!"

He smiles dotingly, but I can tell from his expression that he's already well aware of the reasons I keep tagging along with him. "I'm sure I will. So you know Celine DuFort?"

"Yes, but from a long time ago. Back then, she was a party girl. We all were. From what I remember, which isn't much because our nights out make Girls' Night look tame."

Ambrose laughs. "Considering how many of

them I've had to pick you up from, that's saying something."

"Hey, they're not that bad. And those kinds of nights make strong bonds when you're that age. She's nice. Do you know her?"

He shakes his head. "No, I don't think so."

Our conversation is cut short as we approach the group of witnesses. Ambrose holds out his badge and I get the same surge of pride I normally do when he's in this mode. I love seeing him work.

"Hello, I'm Detective Ambrose, this is my consultant, Amethyst of the Gemstone Coven." He gestures to me with his introduction and I hold up my own ID card, feeling rather important while I do. "We want to ask you some questions about the incident, if you're up for it?"

A man breaks away from the crowd, his eyes wide and harrowed. "I'm Tim, Jeremiah is my best friend."

"I'm sorry for your loss," Ambrose says. He gestures to a quieter spot in the spectator stands. "Could we talk a bit?"

"Yes, of course." He looks uncomfortable, but that isn't unusual at this point. And if he's to be believed, his best friend just died in front of him.

I glance over to where Stacey is tending to Jeremiah's body and a lump forms in my throat.

How would I feel if she was the one who had died and I was having to give a witness statement? Suddenly Tim's predicament seems a lot worse.

The three of us make our way over to the stands. Tim doesn't sit down, instead lighting a cigarette instead. "Do you mind?"

"Go for it," Ambrose responds as he pulls out his notebook, though I notice he keeps his distance between him and Tim's smoke. "You're part of the jousting team? Are you a jouster as well?"

"Hell, no. Have you seen the crazy stuff they get up to? No, that's not for me. I'm part of the crew. I help set up, carry weaponry, that sort of thing. A modern-day squire, if you will. Jeremiah is the adrenaline junkie. He loves the thrill, the glory, the bruises and broken bones. Shows them off whenever we're at a bar to impress the ladies, the idiot. Works like a charm too." His eyes widen and a haunted look flits through them as if he's remembered the situation he's ended up in. "Worked. I can't believe he's dead."

I feel for him. It can't be easy to go from knowing someone is alive and living their life the way they want to one moment, and then they're gone soon after.

I flip open my own notebook, feeling rather official when I do, even if I only have it because I've been too lazy to take it out of my handbag after my last case. If I'm feeling more generous to myself, I'd say that it's in there because Ambrose can call on me to consult on a case at any moment, but considering my main job is making wands in the workshop next door to our home, I don't think I can really use that as an excuse.

"Can you run us through what happened before the accident?" I ask.

Tim draws a shaky breath and nods. "We were just doing a practice run to make sure everyone knew what they were doing during the tournament. Well as much as we can do. Obviously, the results aren't rigged or anything. But it can get hectic. Lars and Jeremiah were doing a pass." He gestures in the vague direction of Jeremiah, which I assume must be where they were doing their practice run.

"Which side did Jeremiah start at?" Ambrose asks.

He points. "Over there. I was on the other end, helping Lars get ready. When they entered the list, they charged at each other." His eyes glaze over. "Both their lances hit. It's such a loud clap when they collide, I can never get used to it. Jeremiah got thrown from his saddle and he hit the ground pretty hard. When he didn't get up, I thought it was a joke. He was a bit of a prankster, like that. This isn't how it's supposed to go, you know?" Tim runs a shaky hand through his hair.

I nod, making my own notes even though Ambrose is doing the same. Sometimes we pick up on different parts of the story, and that can make all the difference when we're trying to work out what happened. "What do you know about Lars Baker?" I ask.

"Lars?" Tim sniffles. "Nice bloke, him. He's new to jousting but he's been riding horses his whole life. You can tell from the way he sits in the saddle, he's a natural."

"You say he's new. How long has he been with the team?" Ambrose asks.

"A few months or so," he replies with a shrug.

That makes me frown. "And he's already riding in the tournament? Is that normal?"

Tim takes a long drag from his cigarette and lets the smoke escape. "I don't know, you'd have to ask the Horse Master. She's in charge of arranging the whole thing."

Ambrose nods gratefully. "Thank you, Tim."

"Is that it?" He seems surprised.

I give him a reassuring smile. "We're just trying to establish a timeline at this point, we might need to talk to you in the future about things as they come up."

Ambrose nods along, letting me do this part because people often respond to me better, even if I personally think he's good at it with his commanding voice and his calm demeanour.

"Great, thanks, I guess?" Tim flicks his cigarette away and heads back over to the other witnesses, leaving us to collect our thoughts and prepare ourselves to learn more about jousting.

This is perhaps a little more of a realistic jousting experience than I had planned when we came to the museum today, but I guess there's no going back now, even if I wanted to.

FOUR

WE'VE MANAGED to talk to most of the witnesses by the time Celine returns from interviewing Lars Baker. She heads straight over to where we're sitting in the stands. As she grows closer, it's possible to make out the troubled expression on her face.

She sits down next to me and lets out a loud sigh.

"And?" I prompt. She may not want to tell us anything about the case, and she has every right to decide not to, but she also clearly *wants* to talk about it.

Celine fiddles with her pen, twirling it as she scans her notes. "He seems genuinely distraught and shocked. My gut says he didn't mean to hurt Jeremiah. I don't know enough about jousting and the mortality rate to know if this is an accident or not," Celine says as she looks at the body. "What did you guys find out?"

"Eyewitness reports are pretty consistent," Ambrose replies. "They say the two rode towards each other, had a collision that threw Jeremiah from his saddle. Multiple people thought it was a prank when he didn't get up. Apparently, he was known to be a bit of a jokester and a lady's man."

I nod, checking my own notes. "We spoke to a few people, including Jeremiah's best friend and we discovered some interesting things about Lars Baker. Apparently, he's relatively new and it's unusual that he was already part of the tournament."

Interest flickers through Celine's eyes. "That is interesting. Who decided to put him in the show?"

"The Horse Master," Ambrose replies. "We haven't had a chance to speak to her yet. Her name is Lori."

"Let's change that then," Celine decides firmly. "I take it you want to come?"

"Do wands spew magic?" I ask.

Celine snorts. "Not if you're using them properly, Ames."

"I know my way around a wand," I mutter.

She lets out a bemused laugh, while Ambrose looks a little mortified.

"Because I'm a wandmaker," I blurt unnecessarily. I've been training with wands since well before I met either of them, they both know what I mean.

"If you say so," she jokes. "Coming?"

I jump to my feet, not wanting her to change her mind.

"You never told me what you were doing here," Celine says as we make our way over to the other side of the courtyard where a stocky woman is coordinating horses and people.

"Oh we were here on a date," I say. "Or we were trying to be here on a date. Then we ran into Stacey, sorry, Doctor Barnes."

Celine raises an eyebrow. "A date? So the two of you..." She gestures between us.

Ambrose turns an alarming shade of red. He's not used to people questioning our personal relationship. I guess to the people we work with at the Hull station, it's a given that we're together.

"We live together," I say brightly. "With our dog."

"Wow, I don't know where to start with any of that," Celine jokes. "I always thought you'd end up back with Flora with all the pining you did over her after your breakup."

"I haven't talked to her in years, actually," I

respond. "I wonder how she's doing?"

"She seems well, if the photos online are anything to go by."

I nod, not really knowing how to respond to the talk of my ex-girlfriend when my very-much-now boyfriend is right next to me.

Thankfully, I'm saved from having to come up with anything when we get to where the Horse Master is tending to her herd. I don't even know if it's considered a herd, but I guess this is the right place to ask if the subject comes up.

Celine clears her throat. "Lori?"

The woman barks a few more orders before turning around. "Thought you might want to talk to me. Before you ask, no, this isn't normal." She sounds exasperated, and I have to wonder how many times she's had this conversation in her head before we approached.

"So injuries are uncommon while jousting?" Ambrose asks.

"Oh, no. You won't find a single jouster without injuries," Lori quickly corrects him. "It's an incredibly dangerous and volatile contact sport, Detective. Everyone has bruises, broken bones, concussions, that sort of thing. It's normal, and everyone knows what they're signing up for. But because it's so dangerous, everything is done to avoid fatal harm. So this isn't normal." She waves her hand around the courtyard and her voice cracks. She's clearly much more affected by the situation than she's trying to let on. I wonder if it's for our benefit, or for the other members of the jousting team?

"So people don't usually die while jousting?" I ask, already certain I know the answer. If there were a lot of jousting-related deaths, they wouldn't be able to do it.

"Not nowadays, no. The few fatal instances are almost always due to someone not paying attention," she says.

Celine gives her a piercing look. "Is that what happened today? Someone wasn't paying attention?"

"No! This is a highly choreographed event. It's not a competition, it's a show. We use lances intended to shatter on impact so it's safer for our riders. I drill safety into my riders from the very first lesson." Pain fills her eyes, and her hand shakes slightly until she pulls herself together.

"But it's still dangerous?" I ask.

Lori gives me a withering look. "It's two knights riding on thundering horses with lances pointed at each other, of course it's dangerous. I don't know what happened, but this wasn't my fault."

The sudden hostility is suspicious, and I can tell from Ambrose's neutral expression that he's probably having similar thoughts. He checks his notes and clears his throat. "Lars Baker. He's new, right?"

"Yes, so?" Lori returns.

"Is that normal that he's already in the tournament?" Celine asks.

That instantly sours the Horse Master's face. "What are you implying?"

"Nothing, we just want to know if Lars Baker usually rides against Jeremiah or not," she clears up in a manner that makes it clear she's used to dealing with witnesses like this.

"No, Jeremiah is much more experienced. Look, I'm not proud of this, but Lars begged me to be part of the tournament. Said it was worth a lot to him and I have five kids to take care of."

I exchange a knowing look with Ambrose. "So he bribed you to be on the roster?"

"No, nobody bribed anyone. He just offered me some grocery money. I figured... what's the harm?" Lori mutters, her gaze glued to the body behind us. "I never thought this would happen. Now if you don't mind, I have a lot to tend to now that the show is cancelled."

"Thank you for your time," Celine says briskly,

though I can tell she's not happy with the dismissal before she's ready. I've seen the same expression on her face several times before, though normally because a bartender refused to serve her.

The three of us make our way to a private spot, and I can tell that both of them are thinking hard about the initial take of the crime scene.

I look from detective to detective. "So, what are we thinking? Murder, manslaughter, or complete accident?"

"I wouldn't like to call it yet," Ambrose says. I know him well enough to know he's got his thinking face on, but we're not on our home turf, we can't just run the investigation like we own it.

"I don't know either," Celine says, her gaze flitting back to where Lars Baker is sitting. "Let's see what the autopsy reveals. Doctor Barnes is taking the body back to the morgue, and I'm going to take Lars Baker into the station for an official statement and dive deeper into it. Accident or not, he killed a man. How long are you two in town?"

I glance at Ambrose, trying to figure out how he feels about the whole thing. Helping out for the afternoon is one thing, hopping on the case fully is another. This is supposed to be a trip away from work for us. Murder might be my hobby but it's his job and he needs a break from it.

His hand touches the small of my back. "We're here for the weekend so if you need more assistance, we're happy to tag along"

Celine smiles. "I'd appreciate that. As I said, we're spread thin. Let's pack it all up and take it in."

"Do you have an evidence bag large enough for the lance?" I ask, partly curious, and partly concerned.

"We'll have to roll it in plastic," Celine says. "Not ideal, but it's a start."

I nod.

She pulls her phone out of her pocket and hands it to me. "Put your contact details in and I'll send you the address for the station, and I'll let the front desk know to expect you."

"Thanks, Celine, we appreciate it," I respond.

"I can safely say I never expected to be working together, but I'm glad you're on my team," she says to me. "It'll be just like old times."

"But with less booze and more murder," I joke.

She glances over at the body. "We don't know that it's murder."

But the end of her sentence hangs in the air between us.

Yet.

FIVE

THE PPD FORENSICS building in Leeds isn't as modern as the one we have in Hull. Or at least, it isn't from the outside, but the moment we pass through the doors, I realise that despite only having been in one morgue in my entire life, I know exactly what kind of building we're in. Apparently, they're all the same. It's the smell, the weird mixture of cleaning products and death. I can't say I enjoy it very much. I don't know how Stacey puts up with the smell as much as she does. Or how she and Gabriel can spend so much time in her office. I've been to his, it's much less full of death, though there are just as many chemicals in the forensics department as in the morgue.

"This way," Celine says as she pushes open the door that I assume leads to the examination room.

Sure enough, Stacey is already doing her thing. Maybe that's why the place feels so familiar. Death smell and Stacey. Just like a normal murder. Though I need to try and remember that this might not be that. It could just be a really horrible accident.

"Hey, Stace," I say brightly.

She looks up and smiles. "I just got a real déja vu."

"Me too," I reply.

Celine clears her throat. "Are you ready to give us a report?" she asks Stacey.

"I can give you some preliminary findings, but it's still early days. None of the blood tests have come back."

"Is that not something you can do with..." Celine gestures around.

Stacey raises an eyebrow. "Magic?"

Celine nods. "We normally borrow our forensic pathologist from Bradford," she admits.

"Ah." Stacey nods.

"Are either of them going to explain?" I whisper to Ambrose.

He chuckles. "He's a shifter, I think."

"Mmhmm," Stacey confirms. "A hellhound, I think. He's great at sniffing out poisoning."

"But not good at what you do?" I check.

Stacey lets out a small laugh. "No one is as good at what I do as I am, that's why I'm the one who does it." From anyone else, it would sound like a brag, but not Stacey. Probably because she has the credentials to back it up. Not everyone is capable of running a morgue of their own by the time they're in their early thirties.

Our attention switches to our victim who lays on the slab. His armour and clothing has all been removed and placed to the side, no doubt waiting for Gabriel to come and collect them so he can do his thing. I don't know precisely where his and Stacey's expertise overlap, but they seem to have the process down to a fine art.

Jeremiah looks younger than I expect, and frailer. Bruises cover his body, and from what Stacey has told me on cases before, I can tell that some of them are older than others.

"Are these all from jousting?" I ask, stepping forward in the hope that a closer look will reveal more, but I don't know enough about the body, or about jousting equipment.

"I don't know yet. I've asked Gabriel to help me identify them. He's into watching jousting so he'll be able to help me figure it out." She lets out a light laugh and shakes her head in amusement. "Men and their toys."

"There were some women there too," Ambrose points out.

"They're still hitting each other with sharp sticks," Stacey mutters.

Celine seems less interested in our debate. "Can you tell whether the blow of the lance killed him?"

Stacey straightens, a satisfied expression crossing her face and telling me the answer before she says it. "I can. If I wasn't a necromancer, it would've taken me a while to figure out in what order these were sustained but a little bit of magic helped clear it right up. This fresh bruise at the base of his neck is definitely the last injury and from the pictures, I can see that he suffered a cervical break at C2."

"So the fall from the horse definitely killed him then?" Celine summarises.

Stacey nods. "Yes. Though that doesn't mean there aren't other things at play here. Without the blood tests, we don't know if he was drugged, or drunk, or anything like that."

"And that could have influenced his death?" Celine asks.

"Absolutely. If he was drugged in some way, he might not have been riding as well as normal. You'll know about that better than I do. One of the witnesses will probably have said if he was acting strange," she responds.

"There wasn't anything of note," Ambrose responds.

Stacey nods. "I'll let you know anything else I discover. His armour, clothes, and personal belongings are on the side. They also brought the lances. Gabriel hasn't had a chance to look at them yet, I think he's still overseeing the team at the museum, there was a lot of evidence to collect. So have at it, but remember to wear gloves."

She gestures to a box and I grab the first pair, slipping them on. I don't have to be told twice, snooping through someone's stuff is great. It's even better when it's legal.

I touch the lance, doing my best not to say any of the jokes that are running through my head right now. None of them are appropriate, even if I think they're funny.

"Which one was Jeremiah's?" I ask.

Stacey hums. "The other one."

I frown.

"What is it?" Ambrose asks.

"Jeremiah's lance is a lot more broken than the one Lars was using." It's immediately obvious when I look at them. Lars' lance barely looks used, whereas

Jeremiah's is splintered all the way up. I don't know enough about the sport to make a proper judgement about the implications, which is frustrating to say the least. I wish Gabriel were here to tell us about it.

"I wonder if that means something," Celine says. "We'll have to get an expert to check it out. And we can ask the witnesses to see if they noticed anything when the two of them reached one another. This might be perfectly normal, or it could be something to look into."

I nod and set the lance down, looking over the rest of the armour. It shines brightly in the harsh lights of the morgue. I suppose I did intend to be looking at armour today, though I have to admit that I was thinking more of the kind where the story's told on a plaque next to it, not the kind I need to put the story together for myself.

Ambrose grabs the evidence bag that's been labelled as the contents of Jeremiah's locker and tips it out on a tray. A variety of items clatter out, including a well-used leather wallet, a smartphone, and a crumbled receipt.

I pick it up and smooth it out. "Looks like Jeremiah bought a Ploughman's sandwich this morning and an energy drink."

Ambrose flicks through the wallet. "A little bit of

cash, credit cards, but no pictures of a partner or family."

"His friends did say he was a player," I say.

"Mmm. But that could all be bravado."

Celine tries the phone. "Locked. We'll have to get our tech department to crack it."

"Does it have fingerprint recognition?" I ask, gesturing backwards. "Because we have a perfectly fine thumb right there."

I can feel both detectives look at me and I can't tell if Celine is impressed or mortified by my suggestion. Ambrose definitely looks pleased, but I know he appreciates the way my mind works, otherwise, he wouldn't let me keep tagging along as his consultant.

Stacey doesn't even bat an eye when Celine asks to borrow the victim's hand. She presses his thumb on the scanner and the device vibrates stubbornly, claiming it's not the right fingerprint.

I can't help but feel disappointed. "Aww, I really thought that would work."

"These sensors work through electrical conductivity. The fresher a body, the better it works," Stacey says. "I'm sorry, I should've unlocked his phone while I did my necromancer autopsy."

"Can we try face ID?" Celine says, holding the

phone up over Jeremiah but it doesn't register either. "We might have to open his eyes and move his head to simulate him being alive. Doctor Barnes, if you would?"

Stacey frowns. "A thumbprint is one thing. I'm not sure I'm comfortable with this, especially as it doesn't always work." She looks at Jeremiah's face, and I can almost *hear* the thoughts running through her head. I'm not entirely certain what the necromancer code of ethics is, just that there is one, and that there's no way Stacey is going to go against it. She cares for the dead too much, which is one of the reasons she's so good at what she does.

"Fair enough." Celine steps away and slips the phone back into the evidence bag. "I'll just get IT to deal with it."

I feel bad that my suggestion led to this awkward moment and I turn my attention back to the rest of his belongings. "Is there a chance that his armour is faulty and that's why his fall was deadly?"

Next to me, Ambrose picks up some piece of chainmail, the metal sound grating. "It looks intact but I know nothing about it. It's best to ask an expert's opinion in this case, I think."

Celine nods. "Agreed. I'll put feelers out to see if we can get an impartial expert on it. I know we could ask Lori, but I'm not entirely certain that she's going to tell us the truth."

"I can do it," a familiar voice says from behind me.

I'm not surprised to see Gabriel entering the morgue. The question is whether he's here to collect things, or just here because he wants to see Stacey. Neither of them are very subtle about the amount of time they want to spend with one another, even now they're officially together. It's cute.

"Hey, Gabriel," I say.

"Doctor Rook," Celine says with a nod.

Ah, right. She only knows Stacey and Gabriel in a professional capacity. She hasn't seen Stacey belting out ballads after one too many cocktails, or seen them awkwardly jump away from one another when they think they've been caught being too intimate in the morgue. It's almost strange to be working with someone who isn't exactly a friend. Though I suppose Celine isn't exactly *not* my friend either. We have history, after all.

"Sounds good," Ambrose says, nodding. He stops halfway through handing one of the evidence bags and shoots Celine an apologetic look. "Sorry, I forgot this isn't my case."

I can't even blame him for getting confused. We're so used to dealing with Stacey and Gabriel,

I've never really thought much about them having other cases and potentially other work friends. Other than the people I also work with at the Hull station. I suddenly feel a little jealous.

Luckily, Celine doesn't seem insulted and just shrugs. "It's fine. You can take whatever you need, Doctor Rook. We should go have a chat with Lars Baker now that he's had some time to calm down and process what's happened. I'll see you at the station?" she asks us.

I nod eagerly, glad that she doesn't seem in the slightest bit inclined to remove us from the case. I'm still disappointed that we haven't gotten to see the exhibits we came to visit, but at least today is turning out interesting.

SIX

I FEEL a weird kind of giddy going into a different police station and getting to see how things are run around here. I just have to hope it goes better than it did the last time we were somewhere else. But this is different. We're here because Celine invited us, whereas in Grimsby, they thought we were trying to steal their case. Which I suppose wasn't entirely untrue, but it wasn't our fault there was a serial killer active in both of our jurisdictions.

We head over to the reception desk where a man with visibly longer fangs greets us with an understandably toothy grin.

Interesting. We don't have any vampires working in our station that I'm aware of. Certainly not at the front desk.

Ambrose holds up his badge. "Detective

Ambrose from Hull PPD and consultant Amethyst of the Gemstone Coven. We're helping Detective DuFort on a case."

I find great pleasure in showing off my consultant badge. There's something so satisfying about whipping it out, it makes me feel like a superstar. Maybe because it's something I've always wanted.

Well, that's not entirely true. Technically, what I wanted was a badge just like Ambrose's. Detective Amethyst has a nice ring to it. But now I'm more settled in my life, I realise that being a consultant makes much more sense for me.

Especially as it means less tedious paperwork.

"She said you'd be coming. Sign in, please." He gestures to the tablet propped up on the front of the desk. "She's in the second interrogation room to the left."

"Thanks," I say, smiling at him.

He shrugs and goes back to whatever he was doing before that. Suddenly I feel a swell of affection for my sister and the sunny disposition she brings to her role as receptionist. I already know she's good at her job, but seeing someone who isn't nearly as invested, it's clear *just* how good at her job she is.

The two of us head into the building, and I'm

unsurprised to find it has a familiar feel to it. Citizens clutter up the waiting area, people in uniform go about their day, and the coffee smells just as crappy as ours. I wonder if they have a coffee shop down the road that they like to go to as well. Probably.

Luckily, we don't have to go searching for Celine as she's waiting outside the interrogation room in question. She smiles as we approach, seemingly relieved that we've actually shown up. I suppose that makes sense. We're not officially on the case, so we don't have to if we don't want to.

"Lars Baker is ready," she says after we've exchanged the necessary pleasantries. "If you're up for it, you can join me, Detective Ambrose. Amy, you can observe from the room next door or I can direct you towards the kitchen. We have coffee."

"I'll observe," I say quickly. And not just because I want to avoid the coffee at all costs. Perhaps we should have made a stop to get one before we arrived.

Ambrose's little smile makes it clear he never thought I'd answer any differently. He knows me well.

"All right, I'm sure you know procedure." She gestures to the door next to the interrogation room.

I smile and make my way inside. For a moment,

I'm surprised to find an officer already inside, but it makes sense. The person on the other side is at the very least a killer, even if they're not a murderer.

A surge of pity goes through me as I look at the seemingly distraught young man on the other side of the glass. If this was a genuine accident, he's going to have to go through his life knowing that he took someone's life. I can't imagine what that must be like. Maybe there's a potion of some kind that he can take to make him forget. I'm not sure if I'd be able to do that.

The officer nods to acknowledge me but doesn't seem interested in making small talk. That's fine by me, I don't need distractions. Presumably, Celine briefed him on the fact I would be here, which is nice. It's certainly interesting to see one of my friends from the academy flourishing.

I take a seat and make myself as comfortable as I can on the hard plastic chair. We have the same ones, and they're never pleasant. At least it helps keep me alert.

Celine and Ambrose enter the room and sit down opposite Lars. I watch him intently to try and gauge his reaction to being faced with two detectives.

He's not as hysterical as when we saw him earlier but not in a way that makes me think he's at ease. I don't like to make snap judgements but it's hard to imagine that someone would be bold or stupid enough to murder out in the open like that.

"We're starting the interview. Present are Lars Baker, attending officer Detective Celine DuFort, and Detective Knight Ambrose from the Hull PPD acting in an advisory capacity," Celine says. "You've waived the right to counsel?" she asks Lars.

He gives a slight nod.

"I'm going to need you to say it out loud for the recording," Celine says.

"I don't want a lawyer," Lars murmurs.

Celine flicks through her files. "So, Lars. Run me through what happened again."

The man sniffles. "We arrived at the museum early in the morning. I got suited up and went to where Thunder was waiting for me."

"Thunder is your horse?" Ambrose asks.

"Yes. Well, not mine. But the one I normally ride," Lars answers.

"Did you notice anything out of the ordinary?" Ambrose continues, his voice level and reassuring. Interesting. If I have to guess, I'd say that Ambrose doesn't believe the man in front of him is guilty of murder.

"No, everything seemed normal. I got up on my horse, got my lance, and rode out into the courtyard towards Jeremiah." Lars Baker rubs tight circles on his temples. "I knew something was wrong when my lance hit his shield and he flew out of the saddle. Jeremiah has been doing this for a long time, he shouldn't have been this easy to dismount."

"So it's unusual for someone to fall during jousting?" Celine asks.

"It is during a tournament. Falling is kind of humiliating, people don't want to see that. They want to see the collision, see the lances explode, that kind of thing."

Ambrose nods. "Speaking of tournaments, how did you get your spot? There are plenty of other, more experienced jousters in the team, aren't there?"

The briefest amount of surprise flits over Lars Baker's face. If we weren't in a controlled environment, I almost definitely would've missed it.

Before he can answer, Celine clears her throat. "I want to circle back to the event. Did you know you were riding against Jeremiah?"

Oh, that's annoying. I think Ambrose might be onto something with the angle of how Lars ended up riding in the first place. If this was our case, it would be playing out a little differently.

Lars Baker nods. "Yes, of course. The line-up

was decided long before we got there. There were some last-minute changes but nothing major."

Both Ambrose and Celine say something, talking over each other. A beat of discomfort hangs in the interrogation room and I feel the second-hand awkwardness surge through me. I'm so used to being in sync with Ambrose during interrogations or seeing him with someone he's used to working with, it's strange to witness this.

Celine is the one to speak again. "What's your relationship with Jeremiah? Did you two get along?"

"Yeah, we did. He was a great guy. Kind of like a role model to me." His voice cracks.

"Like a role model, huh? Why?" Celine asks.

"He was good at jousting, had a lot of sway with the ladies. I wanted to be like him," Lars says.

"So why did you kill him?" Celine asks.

Her direct approach is jarring and from here, I can see Ambrose's shoulders tense but it's not like he can say anything.

Lars Baker's eyes widen. "I-I didn't mean to, it was an accident."

"Why did you bribe Lori?" she asks, not skipping a beat.

Lars Baker shifts uncomfortably in his chair. "I don't know what you're talking about."

"We spoke to Lori, she says you paid her to be in the tournament. Why, Lars?" Celine's tone is harsher and firmer than necessary. "Why did you do that?"

"It's not what you think!" The agitation shows in Lars' voice. "I just wanted to look cool in front of Julia, okay? I boasted to her about being a jouster and she wanted to come see me ride. When I asked Lori to be in the tournament, she said no because I'm too inexperienced. That's when I gave her the money. It wasn't about Jeremiah, okay? I didn't care who I was going to ride against."

Ambrose clears his throat. "I believe you, Lars."

So do I but I'm not sure if Celine is convinced, and I'm not sure what to make of her direct approach. They get up to leave and the officer in the room moves, startling me. I'd forgotten he was here already.

I clear my throat and get up to leave, almost dreading what I'm going to find on the other side of the door.

The tension between the two detectives is palpable, and suddenly I feel lucky that I've been relegated to the observation room. I hadn't considered that their interrogation styles would clash and I feel guilty for us jumping on this case without knowing much about Celine. Sure, I knew her, once, but I had no idea what kind of detective she was and whether we'd like working with her.

She lets out a sigh. "Unless we can find a good motivation for him killing Jeremiah, I don't think there's a way we can charge him with murder. Coffee, anyone?"

All I can do is nod, even as my mind is going a mile a minute. I think there are plenty of things we can explore from that interview, but I'm not sure where precisely to start, or whether Celine will see the same things I did in the demeanour of our prime suspect.

Somehow, I think the politics of working with someone new is what's going to make this an interesting case, rather than the fact we're investigating a death-by-lance.

This is not what I expected when we drove over this morning.

SEVEN

I TAKE a sip from my coffee, doing my best not to grimace as I do. It's worse than I thought it would be, and I already know that Ambrose won't be finishing it. He doesn't even always finish *good* coffee. The only thing I've found he'll drink all of so far is chai lattes, but I don't think it's his perfect drink.

One day, I'll find it.

I drink again despite the poor taste. It could be the uncomfortable atmosphere in the break room that's making it so unpalatable. I want to bring up the mismatched energy in the interrogation room but it's not like I'm in a position to do so. Celine doesn't have to let us tag along, it's a courtesy on her part.

Next time, I'll definitely think twice about muscling onto someone else's crime scene. Probably.

"So..." I clear my throat. "According to the Horse Master, jousting accidents are almost never fatal. If I wanted to kill someone, why would I pick a method that's most likely to fail?"

Celine hums and seems to relax a little bit. "That's a fair point. There are plenty of other ways that would be more efficient."

"Especially if he's as inexperienced as he says he is," I point out. "Someone who has been doing this their whole life would probably know exactly where to hit to cause damage. But someone new? Would he have the knowledge or the ability to pull that off?"

Celine sighs. "True. And none of the witness statements suggest that he's lying about that part. What was it they all said?" She looks at Ambrose and I repress a sigh. At least my interjection seems to have soothed over some of whatever is going on between them.

"That he's a good horseman, but an inexperienced jouster," he says.

Celine nods. "He also said his lance hit the shield and from what the other witnesses said, that's true, right?"

Ambrose nods. "Yes, I've been thinking about

that. If Lars Baker wanted to kill Jeremiah, wouldn't he have aimed somewhere else? Like his face?"

"Or his neck," I murmur.

Both of them look at me.

I shrug. "When I was reading up about the museum, I read about armour and it said that the weak spots are anywhere where there's a joint. So the neck, the elbows, shoulders, knees. You get the picture. Some people who were riding into actual battle would have witches enchant those spots in order to protect them further. I didn't feel anything magical on the armour, but I'm sure Gabriel — Doctor Rook will be able to tell us if there's anything going on there."

Celine nods. "Interesting."

Ambrose gives me a small smile that I read as pride. He's always impressed with the information I can retain, and the fact that I can apply it to cases.

"Anyway, surely if he was aiming to kill, or even to wound, that's where he'd have gone for. But for the tournament, they *want* to aim for the shield, and that's what he did."

Ambrose hums. "So what you're saying is that you think Lars was doing things exactly the way he was supposed to?"

"It looks that way. But maybe there's more to it?"

Celine sighs. "Why can't these things ever be easy?"

Ambrose chuckles. "They certainly like to make us work for the resolution."

"What about motive? Do we have a good motivation why Lars wants Jeremiah dead? Without one, it sounds like a genuine accident," I summarise.

Celine shrugs. "Motivations don't have to be good, they just have to make sense. But yeah, you've got a point. And a jury will think so too." She sighs, and I recognise the expression on her face from when I've seen one of the detectives at home struggle with a break in the case. And I've probably pulled it myself a few times.

I feel unsatisfied with that answer. "A few people have mentioned that it's weird that Jeremiah fell. Could it be that something was wrong with his saddle? Maybe someone tampered with it?"

"That's possible. We won't know until the expert has examined all the pieces, the armour, and the lances. Oh hang on, I'm getting a call." She gets up from the seat, abandoning her half-empty mug of coffee so she can take the call in the privacy of the hallway.

I watch her, feeling a weird sense of being left out. I'm far too used to the casualness with which Ambrose lets me listen in to these things. And it's not just him either, it's the forensics team, and Detectives Perry and Dean. All of them would want my opinion.

The door falls shut behind her, giving Ambrose and me a moment to ourselves. I reach out to him now that we're alone. "Are you okay?"

He nods and smiles. "Yes, don't worry about me. This isn't the first time I've butted heads with someone in an interrogation. This was mild compared to some of the other people I've worked with."

"Really?"

"Yes. I didn't have a partner for a good reason. Besides, everyone has their own interrogation styles. I don't actually think she did anything wrong, I just would've liked to know beforehand that she didn't want to skirt around the topic." He gives me a curious look. "What do you think about this case? Do you think we've got a murder on our hands?"

"I don't know. The bribing looks bad, but I don't get killer vibes from Lars Baker. If he wanted to get rid of Jeremiah, and that's a big if, there are so many easier ways. I mean, not *easier* but I mean with a better success rate."

Ambrose nods. "I agree. It seems like a dumb method and he seems genuinely distressed that he's caused a death."

"So no jousting murder, just jousting accident?"

He chuckles. "No need to sound so disappointed."

"I'm not," I deny quickly. "Okay, maybe a little. I'm also a bit sad that we didn't actually get to look at old stuff or see the jousting for ourselves. You know how much I like a man who knows how to handle a rod of wood."

Ambrose groans.

"Oh please, you're a mage, and I've seen you handling your staff, you know exactly what I'm talking about." I raise an eyebrow for added effect.

Ambrose gives me a bemused but affectionate look. "Are you ever going to run out of staff jokes?"

"Never. They're one of the reasons you fell for me."

The door opens before he can respond, and Celine returns with her laptop in hand.

"That was the jousting expert," she says.

"That was quick," I muse.

"That's what I thought, but it turns out that Doctor Rook is well-connected and managed to get us someone who was available, local, and intrigued. Anyway, he said one of the lances didn't have the right tip. I don't know the actual specifics, but he mentioned that lances for this kind of show and tournament usually have tips that are usually made from..." She checks her notes. "Balsa wood. It's supposed to shatter more easily. Sometimes, they're partially cut to make it even easier."

I nod, thinking back to how Jeremiah's lance had looked. That one clearly had a balsa wood tip. "Right, for the crowd."

Celine nods. "Yes, but the tip on Lars Baker's lance was hardwood. It hits with much more force and isn't recommended for actual jousting, but is more in line with lances that would be taken into battle, or are just for show."

"I didn't realise there was a difference," Ambrose says. I can tell from his face that he's full of thoughts. "Are the spears easily mistakeable?"

"The expert said it's easy for him to tell, but a novice or someone in a rush could've easily mistaken them."

The implication silences the room for a moment.

Ambrose sits back with a sigh. "So that explains why Jeremiah got unsaddled. He was hit with a much greater force than he expected. Combine that with an unlucky fall, and there we have it."

Celine finishes the rest of her coffee which is no doubt cold. "Doesn't tell us if it's an accident or not.

Even if he did it on purpose, without a good motive, I don't think we can make it stick."

"So if Lars Baker did this, he might get away with it?" I say, my gut twisting tight. This is not the outcome I was expecting.

"We'll keep looking into Jeremiah's life and see if we can find a motive. I'll talk to his friends, coworkers, and family, see if we can find any reason why Lars Baker might've wanted to kill him. Although all of that can wait after lunch." Celine cracks her neck. "Do you want any recommendations on where to go? I know the city well."

"That'd be great," I say.

"We can come back after lunch to help with the interrogations if you want?" Ambrose offers.

I watch Celine's face, hoping that the near-altercation in the interrogation room isn't going to have put her off from wanting us to help more. If Ambrose is telling the truth about it being the norm, then there's nothing to really worry about. And I don't think he'd have a reason to lie.

Relief flashes over Celine's face and I wonder if she was worried about us not wanting to help. "That'd be great, thanks. It's a lot of witnesses to deal with on my own, and as much as I know the uniforms could do a decent job, it's not the same as having an experienced detective helping."

"Great, then we'll grab some lunch and come back," he says. "What do you fancy?" he asks me.

"Kebabs."

Celine laughs. "Please tell me it's not because you've been thinking of things being skewered?"

I shrug. "Huh, maybe."

She shakes her head in bemusement. "Well, you're in luck. There's a great food market a few streets down that has a stall with some good kebabs, I'll ping you the address."

"Thanks." I smile and get to my feet, realising that I'm actually starving.

And looking forward to the rest of my day. But then again, good food and murder-solving. What's not to love?

EIGHT

THERE'S a quiet calmness to walking through the bustling city with Ambrose's hand in mine. It feels so delightfully mundane and boring to stroll around like we have no worries and there aren't people hurting others somewhere behind closed doors.

I say while we're investigating a suspicious death, but that's just normal for us.

The smell of fresh pastries catches my attention and I sniff around for their direction.

Ambrose chuckles. "You look like Rover when you do that."

I exaggerate and put my nose even more in the air. "It smells like puff pastry. Maybe croissants?"

His arm slips around me. "We can have all the croissants you want. Though I thought you wanted kebabs?"

"This is a holiday, I can have both," I joke.

"Is it a holiday if we're in a city an hour and a half from home and we're working a case?" he asks.

"It's a holiday if we count it as one," I counter, grinning when we reach a lovely food market with all sorts of stalls. This is exactly the kind of thing that we like and we're allowed some treats.

My nose finds the stall that smells so good that has a variety of baked goods on sale. My mouth waters and my stomach rumbles at the sight of them and without thinking I end up buying one of each, much to Ambrose's bemusement.

"What if we end up interviewing witnesses all night and we need sustenance?" I ask.

"I didn't say anything," he responds. "And I know you'll be eating at least three of them for breakfast tomorrow."

"I will not." Maybe. It depends what else we buy.

It doesn't take long for me to fill up the reusable shopping bag we brought with us with all kinds of treats to take home, including some delicious nutty cheese for Grammie, a fancy dog treat for Rover, and some liquor chocolates for Topaz and Steve. I don't know if he'll enjoy them, but I know my sister will, and her happiness seems to be the most important thing to her husband.

We finally find the kebab stand that Celine told us about and order a selection of items to eat while we continue walking around the market. We don't get to visit these places nearly often enough.

I finish off the final chicken cubes and throw the skewer into the nearby bin, cleaning off my hands with a napkin.

"How long have we got?" I ask Ambrose.

He hums and pulls out his phone to check it. "We should go back to the station now, Celine says the best friend has just come in to answer more questions."

"That's all right. Murder is more fun than pastries." I lace my arm through his.

"It might not be murder," he reminds me.

"I know, but *manslaughter is more fun than pastries* doesn't have the same ring to it, makes it sound like I'm going around killing people by accident."

He raises an eyebrow. "You have an interesting outlook on life."

"And you love it."

"I love you," he responds earnestly.

"Well, you're in luck, 'cause I love you too." I lean in and kiss his cheek. It feels like we're breaking some kind of rule because we're in the middle of a case.

Unsurprisingly, the short walk back to the

station is uneventful, even laden down with all of the produce.

"Pass the bag?" I ask Ambrose the moment we're inside.

He frowns and does as I ask. "Why?"

I check around to make sure no one is looking and then pull my wand from the specially designed pocket. I tap it against the bag, making it shrink in size until it's small enough to put in my handbag.

"You couldn't have done that before?"

"Too many humans around," I respond, slipping it into my bag. "But at least we don't have to meet a load of witnesses looking like we've just been to a farmer's market."

"We have."

"But that doesn't mean we have to let them know that." I put my wand away, knowing that I'm not going to need it.

I nod to the vampire behind the front desk, but he barely even acknowledges us. Which is a shame, I'd have loved another chance to flash my consultant badge at him. I'd use it to buy groceries if I could.

Celine emerges from what I presume is her office, sighing with relief as her eyes land on us. "Hey, welcome back."

"It already feels like home," I joke.

"Yeah, all the stations look the same, don't

they?" Celine gestures at one of the visitation rooms. "We've got Tim in there, I thought maybe he could help shed some light on any potential conflicts between Jeremiah and Lars Baker."

I frown. "There's something I've been wondering about. The hardwood tip."

Ambrose lets out a choked snort.

"I'm not making a joke," I chastise him. "On purpose or not, why didn't the person handing him the lance not notice that it had the wrong tip? And if they didn't notice, maybe that means something."

"Interesting point. We should find out who that was and ask them. The answer should be interesting." Celine nods. "Shall we?"

Ambrose touches the small of my back on the way in, a small affectionate gesture. I'm surprised I'm not relegated to the observation room again, but I suppose we're not questioning a suspect this time.

The three of us sit opposite of Tim who only seems marginally more together. He's certainly nowhere near as distraught as Lars is, but I suppose Tim isn't the one who killed anyone.

"Thank you for coming in, Tim," Celine says. "We were hoping you could fill in some blanks for us about Jeremiah."

Tim nods shakily. "Yes, of course. Anything I

can do to help. Jeremiah was like a brother to me. What do you need to know?"

"Did he know Lars Baker well?" Celine asks.

"Lars? Umm... I don't think so. Lars was a bit of a show-off, thought he was better than everyone cause he comes from money. Bragged about all the horses he used to own as a child. Not really our type of guy."

"So they didn't hang out?" I ask at the same time as Celine speaks. I shoot her an apologetic smile.

Three is definitely a crowd.

Tim shrugs. "Not outside work, no. Why? Why are you asking about Lars? I thought this was an accident."

"We're still trying to figure that out." Celine's phone beeps and she clears her throat. "Detective, Amethyst, a moment, please?"

I rise, eager to find out what that's about.

Out in the hallway, Celine makes sure to close the door properly before she speaks, her voice lowered. "IT managed to unlock Jeremiah's phone and found something interesting."

I perk up. Now this is the good stuff.

She turns her phone to show us a woman in daring lingerie.

I can feel my cheeks heat up. "I think those are private pictures."

Celine shakes her head. "Those were on Jeremiah's phone. There are lots of them too, all the same woman. Some of them aren't sexy either, just them being cute together."

I hum. "That's weird. Tim called Jeremiah a ladies man. As his best friend, why didn't he know Jeremiah had a girlfriend?"

"I have an answer for that," Celine says, swiping to the next picture. "IT ran a reverse image search for the woman and we found her social media profile. You're looking at Rachel Sanders, also known as the wife of Tim Sanders."

I glance at Ambrose and see my own shock written on his face just as plainly. This isn't what I expected them to find on his phone.

"Okay, so that would explain why Tim didn't know about Jeremiah's girlfriend," I say. "Almost sounds like he has more of a motive than Lars does for this."

Ambrose frowns.

"You've remembered something?" I ask.

Celine watches us with interest, probably realising that while this is her case, the two of us are so used to working together that we've got a natural shorthand going on between us. Or she realises that's the case because we're together, but we make an effort not to be too coupley when we're on a case.

It's one of the reasons I made sure to shrink the bag of goodies.

"I think so," Ambrose murmurs as he reaches for his notebook. "When we talked to him, he said he was a modern-day squire. He helps set up and *carry weaponry.*"

Celine's eyes widen as the implication hits home.

Tim doesn't just have the motive, he also had the opportunity, and the same can't be said for Lars.

"Is it possible that *he* gave Lars Baker the wrong lance?" Celine murmurs.

I turn my gaze towards the visitation room. "I think we may have just found the real killer."

And now comes the hard bit.

We have to prove it.

NINE

Tim is leaning back in his chair when we re-enter the room, clearly not even slightly concerned about what we've worked out.

Then again, I suppose he thinks it's a secret.

Tension hangs in the room, but it's different from before. Ambrose and Celine sit down at the table while I remain standing a little further back wondering if I should be in the observation room now we're going to be interviewing a suspect rather than a witness. I push the thought to the side. Celine would have no problem with asking me to go there, and I know Ambrose probably wants me here in case I make some kind of observation that will help us break Tim.

I lean back against the wall, grateful that at least I have some space. With the two detectives sitting at the table already, there admittedly isn't much of it. Yet another reason to be grateful that Ambrose doesn't have an official detective partner, though he does sometimes work with Perry or Dean on cases. Most of the time though, it's just the two of us. Solving crimes, then going to the beach to walk our dog. It's the dream life.

I dismiss the thoughts from my mind and focus on the scene in front of me.

Celine puts her file on the table and clears her throat. "Tim, how long have you been a member of the jousting team?"

"About... Seven years or so? It was actually Jeremiah's idea," Tim replies.

Ambrose checks his notebook. "When we spoke initially, you called yourself a modern-day squire. Were you the one who handed Lars Baker his lance?"

"Ummm... I don't remember," Tim replies, seeming a little flustered.

"You don't remember whether you handed the lance to the man who killed your best friend? I thought you said that was your job?" Celine's voice is calm but sharp at the same time. Unlike last time, I think it's needed though. Tim is going to respond better to the accusations.

Probably because there's actually something to accuse him of.

Tim's leg starts bouncing. "My memories are a bit hazy, I think it's from the shock."

Suspicious. I resist the urge to say anything. This isn't Ambrose's case, so I shouldn't interfere. And from the expression on Celine's face, there's no need to. She's already onto him.

Ambrose flicks through his notes. "Tim, do you know the difference between a balsa wood tip and a hardwood tip?"

"Ummm, yes, of course. It's my job to know these things," Tim replies.

An idea comes to me and I lean forward to whisper in Ambrose's ear. "Ask him if he'd be able to tell the difference if he saw them."

Ambrose gives a slight nod and clears his throat. "Would you be able to tell them apart on sight?" Ambrose asks.

"I've been doing this for years, what do you think?" Tim responds defensively.

"Answer the question, please Mr Sanders," Celine says firmly.

"Yes, I can tell the difference. It's obvious if you know what you're looking for." He crosses his arms.

Interesting. I wonder if he knows what he's just

admitted. Maybe he thinks we won't have enough information to put the pieces together ourselves.

Celine opens her file and puts a freshly-printed picture of Rachel in lingerie on the table.

The colour drains from Tim's face instantly. "What's this?"

"We found it on Jeremiah's phone," Celine replies, her voice calm and factual. "Were you aware that your best friend was sleeping with your wife?"

"N-No," Tim denies as he pushes the photo back. "No, this is new to me."

"Are you sure?" Ambrose says, his voice slightly harder than it normally is.

Which means that he thinks Tim is definitely lying. I've been in enough interrogations with Ambrose to be able to tell what he's thinking by the tone of his voice.

Celine hums. "It's not easy to hide an affair, especially not from someone close to you. Are you saying you had no idea?"

Tim shakes his head almost desperately. "No, I didn't know anything about this at all."

Now Ambrose isn't the only one who is going to be certain about the lie. Tim couldn't be more obvious about it if there was a neon sign hanging over his head and lit up with magic.

Celine's expression hardens. "I don't think so,

Tim. I think you knew exactly what Jeremiah and your wife were doing. How did you find out? Did she become distant? Did you find the messages on her phone? Did you walk in on them?"

"No, no, nothing like that!" Tim practically presses his hands over his ears, trying to silence the world.

"How did it happen then?" Ambrose prompts.

"He got really drunk a few nights before the tournament and I ordered a taxi through his phone. A message popped up with an image and I saw her picture, *that* picture..." Tim's gaze flits back to the picture and the dam breaks. Tears stream down his cheeks as he rocks back and forth. "He was my best friend. She's my *wife.*"

Even if he potentially murdered said best friend, I can't help but feel sorry for the man on the other side of the coffee table. Killer or not, this kind of betrayal would be hard for anyone to take. And he's lost everything in a matter of moments. I doubt his wife is going to forgive him after this.

Celine clears her throat. "You were upset, hurt, betrayed. I can understand that. Is that why you swapped out the balsa wood tip for hardwood?"

Tim's hands start to shake. "I didn't mean for him to fall like that. I just wanted to hurt him so he knew how I felt. I didn't know he would die. He's fallen off his damn horse so many times before, it never... I didn't... I swear, I didn't mean for this to happen. I'm sorry, I'm so sorry." He buries his face in his hands, but not before I see the despair written all over his face.

This isn't a stone-hearted killer. This is probably someone who made a bad decision at the wrong moment. If Jeremiah hadn't died, the police would never have been called and no one would have ever known the truth about what's going on between the two of them. But sympathy isn't going to save him from the repercussions. Even if he didn't mean for Jeremiah to die, he did. That'll upgrade the charges from manslaughter to second-degree murder.

If he's lucky, he might get a plea bargain that takes it back down, but nothing about Tim Sanders seems lucky right now. He's lost his best friend through his own doing, no doubt he'll lose his wife and his freedom over this too. I can't say it's been a very good day for him.

His sobs fill the quiet room and I can feel my chest tighten from the raw emotion. I have no doubt that he's truly regretful about what happened but that doesn't change the fact that his actions killed a man. Unsurprisingly, I don't feel the same sense of relief I do when I know we've gotten someone truly bad off the streets. I just feel bad for this man. If there hadn't been a lance and the power of horses behind, he wouldn't be in this position.

But I guess that's the hard part of this. He still has the ability to kill even if he didn't have the intention to. I don't think it really matters though, no punishment we give this man is going to be anything compared to the guilt he's feeling. He's going to live the rest of his life trapped by this knowledge, and it'll eat him up.

I just hope he gets the help he needs to move past this.

TEN

As the afternoon turns into evening, the station becomes almost eerily quiet. The day shift workers are making their way home, and the civilians are going back to their normal lives. There's always something nice about this time.

I rest my hand on Ambrose's knee as we sit in the waiting area. We're not needed for the official confession and all the paperwork, but it seems impolite to just skip out without saying a proper goodbye. Especially as it was a courtesy on Celine's part that we were even able to help with the case.

My phone vibrates in my purse and I pull it out, realising I haven't checked it in hours. I should have been paying more attention, but everyone we know is aware that we're away for the weekend.

A message from Grammie waits in the

notification bar and it takes me to our chat where numerous pictures of Rover are waiting for us. Just seeing his floppy ears and adorable snout make me warm and fuzzy.

"Aww, look how cute he is." I hold out the phone for Ambrose to look through the photos.

He leans closer and I can smell his reassuring and familiar scent. His smile brightens his face. "Such a good boy. Looks like he's been asleep most of the day."

"Of course, that's his favourite thing to do. Lazy dog," I say, the affection clear in my voice. It's not hard, Rover is the cutest pet I've ever had but that's not something I'll ever admit out loud in case Herbert hears me. Though he's safely back at the wand shop, my secret is probably safe. Though I don't know, sometimes the gargoyle just seems to *know* things.

I smile when Ambrose takes my hand in his. These small gestures of intimacy are my favourite. It's strange to think that we were strangers a few years ago, and now he's the person I want to be around more than anyone else.

"I'm ready to go home," I confess, looking forward to seeing Rover again, and to being able to spend time just the three of us. Maybe with some good takeaway food and a fun show on the TV. It sounds perfect.

"Me too," Ambrose agrees. "Though I'm glad I still got to spend lots of time with you this weekend."

"That's because you'd spend every day with me if you could. Oh wait, you do." I kiss his cheek.

He chuckles. "Well, you might not have long to wait until hometime. Celine just came out." He gets up and dusts off his hands, though I'm not sure precisely what he's cleaning off them.

I follow suit, smiling when the other detective reaches us.

Celine holds out her hand. "That's this case officially solved. I got a signed confession and everything. Thank you for helping me out. It was a pleasure."

"Thanks for letting us tag along and satiating our curiosity," Ambrose returns, shaking firmly. "Amy would've been speculating all weekend otherwise."

I laugh. "So true."

Celine chuckles. "I remember what she's like when she gets a notion in her head. I don't envy you, Detective Ambrose."

"I wouldn't want her any other way," he says with an affectionate smile.

"Mmm, I remember that too. Amy has a way of making people like her."

"Why do I feel like that's some kind of insult?" I murmur.

Ambrose chuckles and touches my lower back while Celine stretches her hand out to me.

"It wasn't," she assures me as she shakes my hand. "It was great to see you again. A change of pace compared to our nights out but a nice change."

"I agree. Murder is much more exciting than dancing on bars." I glance back to the interview room where Tim is being advised by his lawyer. "What's going to happen to him and Lars Baker?"

"You'll probably have worked it out already, but Tim will be charged with second-degree murder because he actually meant for Jeremiah to get hurt, but I don't think it'll stick in court, especially if he gets a good lawyer. I wouldn't be surprised if that one ends up as a manslaughter plea bargain," she says. "Especially as he seems remorseful."

Ah, so what I thought. It's reassuring in a strange way. I suppose because I know what I'm talking about, and also because it means he won't be charged the same as someone who purposefully goes out to try and kill someone.

"And Lars?" I ask.

"Likely nothing. He was just unlucky, wrong

place, wrong time. I wouldn't be surprised if he gives up jousting." Celine sighs. "Just a lose-lose situation all around."

"Murder tends to be like that."

Celine chuckles. "Yes, it does. So what are your plans now?"

I look at Ambrose and smile. "I think we're headed home. Our dog is waiting for us and I think I've had enough excitement for the weekend."

"So you don't want to visit the museum anymore?" Celine asks.

"What? No, I do! But it's still closed."

She chuckles. "I called in a favour. If you're up for it, the two of you can go on a private tour of the museum tonight."

I let out a small squeal of excitement then remember where we are.

Ambrose's arm wraps around me. "Looks like we're staying a bit longer then. We are on holiday after all and I'm intrigued by the elephant armour."

Gratitude surges through me. "I really want to see those old wands. Thank you, Celine. That's really thoughtful."

"No worries, my way of saying thanks. I don't like working without a partner, things tend to slip through the cracks." She nods. "So yeah, thank you."

"Let me know if you're ever out our way, right?" I check.

"I definitely will be doing," she responds. "Keep in touch?"

"Absolutely." I don't know if we'll actually manage to make that a reality, but part of adult life seems to be promising people you'll talk again, even if you don't know for sure.

We say goodbye with a wave and the vague promise that we'll do it again sometime. I'm not sure if that'll ever happen but I'm pleased to know that no matter where we go, Ambrose and I are a good team.

"So, ancient wands, enchanted helmets, and elephant armour?" Ambrose checks.

"Sounds like a good date to me," I say, almost skipping despite how tired I am. "I hope you realise that I'm going to tell you *everything* I learned in preparation for this trip."

"And I hope you realise that I was hoping you'd do that. I'm sorry we won't get to see the jousting tournament."

"That's okay, I think I've had enough of jousting to last a lifetime."

Ambrose chuckles. "I give it a year, then you'll want to come back."

"Maybe." But I'm not so sure. I don't think I'll

ever be able to ignore the tragedy of this case when I see jousting. But I guess time will tell.

For now, I'm going to focus on the other cool things the museum has to show us and enjoy my moment of peace before we're thrown back into solving murders.

THANK you for reading *Lances and Chances*, we hope you enjoyed it! If you want to learn more about how Amy and Ambrose met, and some of the cases mentioned in the story, you can start the series with *Hexes and Vexes*: https://books2read.com/hexesandvexes

Or, if you're interested in finding out more about Stacey and Gabriel's forensic skills (and necromancy!) you can check out *Grave Mistake*: https://books2read.com/stacey1

AUTHOR NOTE

Thank you for reading *Lances and Chances*, we hope you enjoyed it!

We wrote this side story for the series because of the 2023 book signing event at the Leeds Armouries. The museum is one that Laura visited a good number of times as a child (having grown up nearby) and we knew that we wanted to attend the signing the moment the venue was announced. And then we started thinking - why not have Amy and Ambrose also visit? And then the pieces start slotting into places. With all the demonstrations going on at the museum, there was a murder mystery staple that we haven't done in the main series yet that would work perfectly - the mediaeval reenactment accident. And so Lances and Chances was born!

If you're wanting to know where this fits into the main series, it's set between *Spells and Bells* (book 8) and *Trials and Vials* (book 9), which is also after Stacey and Gabriel's book, *Grave Mistake*.

Several of the murders and cases the characters mention during *Lances and Chances* already appear in the series, including "two bodies, one coffin" (*Grave Mistake*), the Frankenstein body (*Witches and Stitches*), the serial killer across both Grimsby and Hull (*Rhymes and Crimes*) and the wedding cake baker (*Spells and Bells*.)

We do intend for Celine to appear in the main series, but she is a new introduction in *Lances and Chances*!

You can keep up to date with us in several ways: on Laura's Mailing List, on Arizona's Mailing List, in Laura's Reader Group, and in Arizona's Reader Group.

Stay Safe & Happy Reading,

Laura & Arizona

ALSO BY LAURA GREENWOOD

Signed Paperback & Merchandise:

You can find signed paperbacks, hardcovers, and merchandise based on my series (including stickers, magnets, face masks, and more!) via my website: https://www.authorlauragreenwood.co.uk/p/shop.html

Series List:

* denotes a completed series

The Obscure World

A paranormal & urban fantasy world where supernaturals live out in the open alongside humans. Each series can be read on its own, but there are cameos from past characters and mentions of previous events.

Ashryn Barker* - Grimalkin Academy: Kittens* - Grimalkin Academy: Catacombs* - City Of Blood* - Grimalkin Vampires* - Supernatural Retrieval Agency* - The Black Fan - Sabre Woods Academy* - Scythe Grove Academy* - The Shifter Season - Cauldron Coffee Shop - Broomstick Bakery - Obscure Academy - Stonerest Academy - Obscure World: Holidays - Harker Academy

***

The Forgotten Gods World

A fantasy romance world based on Egyptian mythology. Each series can be read on its own, but there are cameos from past characters and mentions of previous events.

The Queen of Gods* - Forgotten Gods - Forgotten Gods: Origins*

***

The Egyptian Empire

A modern fantasy world set in an alternative timeline where the Egyptian Empire never fell.

The Apprentice Of Anubis

***

The Grimm World

A fantasy fairy tale romance world. Each series can be

read on its own, but there are cameos from past characters and mentions of previous events.

Grimm Academy* - Fate Of The Crown* - Once Upon An Academy* - The Princess Competition

The Paranormal Council World

A paranormal romance & urban fantasy world where paranormals are hidden away from the human world, and are in search of their fated mates. Each series can be read on its own, but there are cameos from past characters and mentions of previous events.

The Paranormal Council Series* - The Fae Queens* - Paranormal Criminal Investigations* - MatchMater Paranormal Dating App* - The Necromancer Council* - Return Of The Fae*

Other Series

Beyond The Curse* - Untold Tales* - The Dragon

Duels* - Rosewood Academy - ME* - Speed Dating With The Denizens Of The Underworld (shared world) - Seven Wardens* (co-written with Skye MacKinnon) - Tales Of Clan Robbins (co-written with L.A. Boruff) -

Firehouse Witches* (co-written with Lacey Carter Andersen & L.A. Boruff) - Purple Oasis (co-written series with Arizona Tape) - Valentine Pride* (co-written with L.A. Boruff) - Magic and Metaphysics Academy* (co-written with L.A. Boruff)

Twin Souls Universe

A paranormal romance & urban fantasy world co-written with Arizona Tape. Each series can be read on its own, but there are cameos from past characters and mentions of previous events.

Twin Souls* - Dragon Soul* - The Renegade Dragons* - The Vampire Detective* - Amethyst's Wand Shop Mysteries - The Necromancer Morgue Mysteries

ALSO BY ARIZONA TAPE

Here are some recommendations on some of my other books you might like. My books are available on all retailers and can be requested in most public libraries.

You can find out more about each of my series on my website.

Crescent Lake Shifters

Take a leap of faith with these dragon shifters looking for love. Only a jump in the Crescent Lake will reveal the bonds of fate. A paranormal romance series. Each book follows a different couple.

The Griffin Sanctuary

Help Charlotte take care of endangered mythical animals in the Griffin Sanctuary in this urban fantasy series. Perfect for animal and mythology lovers.

Queens Of Olympus

A modern paranormal romance take on the Greek gods and their dating life; it's not *all* drama. Each book follows a different couple.

The Forked Tail

Get hungry with this urban fantasy series following demon chef Lana and gluttony demon Demi who cook and eat sin for breakfast, lunch, and dinner.

Crescent Lake Bears

Jump in the lake of love with these bear shifters looking for their fated mates. Only the crescent moon will reveal what's meant to be. A paranormal romance series. Each book follows a different couple.

Amethyst's Wand Shop Mysteries

An urban fantasy murder mystery series following a witch who teams up with a detective to solve murders. Each book includes a different murder.

Aliens And Animals

Get accidentally abducted in this Sci-Fi romance series and enjoy the miscommunication, cute animals, and charming aliens. Each book includes a different couple.

Purple Oasis

Find love and hope after the apocalypse at a sanctuary for witches, shifters, and more in this paranormal romance series. Each book follows a different couple.

For a full comprehensive list of all my books: www.

arizonatape.com/all-series

Signed Paperback & Merchandise:

You can find signed paperbacks, hardcovers, and merchandise based on my series (including stickers, magnets, badges, and more!) via my website: www.arizonatape.com/shop

My website also has a selection of free stories and books that'll give you a taste of my other works: www.arizonatape.com/free

ABOUT LAURA GREENWOOD

Laura is a USA Today Bestselling Author of paranormal, fantasy, urban fantasy, and contemporary romance. When she's not writing, she drinks a lot of tea, tries to resist French macarons, and works towards a diploma in Egyptology. She lives in the UK, where most of her books are set. Laura specialises in quick reads, whether you're looking for a swoonworthy romance for the bath, or an action-packed adventure for your latest journey, you'll find the perfect match amongst her books!

Follow the Author

- Website: www.authorlauragreenwood.co.uk
- Mailing List: www.authorlauragreenwood.co.uk/p/mailing-list-sign-up.html
- Facebook Group: http://facebook.com/groups/theparanormalcouncil

- Facebook Page: http://facebook.com/authorlauragreenwood
- Bookbub: www.bookbub.com/authors/laura-greenwood

ABOUT ARIZONA TAPE

Arizona Tape lives her dream life hanging out with her dog and writing stories all day.

Her favourite books to write are urban fantasy and paranormal romances with queer leads, stories that she wished were around when she was younger.

When she's not writing, she can be found cooking up a storm in the kitchen, watching shows that make her cry, or trying her hand at her new hobby of the week.

She currently lives in the United Kingdom with her girlfriend and her adorable dog who is the star of her newsletter.

Sign up here for adorable pictures, free books, and news about her books: www.arizonatape.com/subscribe

Follow Arizona Tape

- Website: www.arizonatape.com
- Mailing List: www.arizonatape.com/subscribe
- Facebook Page: http://facebook.com/arizonatapeauthor
- Reader Group: http://facebook.com/groups/arizonatape
- Bookbub: http://www.bookbub.com/authors/arizona-tape
- Twitter: http://twitter.com/arizonatape
- Instagram: http://instagram.com/arizonatape
- TikTok: http://www.tiktok.com/@arizonatape

Printed in Great Britain
by Amazon